like it. She is small,
funny, clever,
sneaky and musical.
Before she became a writer, she wanted to be a
champion ballroom dancer or a jockey, but she
was actually a lifeguard at a swimming pool,
a radio newsreader, a cleaner in an old people's
home, and a juggler. She likes Marmite on toast
for mains breakfast, and jam on toast for
pudding. Her perfect day would involve baking,
surfing, sitting in cafes in Paris, and playing
with her daughter – who reminds her
a lot of Penny Dreadful…

Jess Mikhail

illustrated this book.
She loves creating funny
characters with bright
colours and fancy
patterns to make people smile.

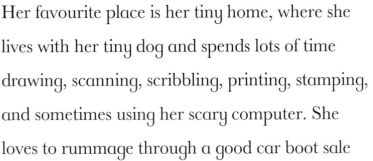

Her favourite place is her tiny home, where she
lives with her tiny dog and spends lots of time
drawing, scanning, scribbling, printing, stamping,
and sometimes using her scary computer. She
loves to rummage through a good car boot sale
or a charity shop to find weird and
wonderful things. A perfect day for
her would have to involve a sunny
beach and large amounts of curry
and ice cream (not together).

Penny Dreadful

and the

Rat

By Joanna Nadin
Illustrated by Jess Mikhail

Meet Penny Dreadful and her Resigned Relations

Penny
(It's never really her fault…)

Cosmo
(Penny's best friend)

Georgia May Morton-Jones
(Penny's clever cousin)

Daisy
(Penny's annoying sister)

Penny's
long-suffering **mum** and **dad**

Very prim-and-proper
Aunt Deedee

Barry
(Miaow, I'm Gran's cat)

Gran
(Normally found fast asleep somewh...)

My name is not actually Penny Dreadful. It is Penelope Jones.

The "Dreadful" bit is my dad's **JOKE**. I know it is a joke because every time he says it he laughs like a honking goose. But I do not see the funny side.

Plus it is not even true that I am dreadful. It is like Gran says, i.e. that I am a **MAGNET FOR DISASTER**. Mum says if Gran kept a better eye on me in the first place instead of on *Paper Doily* in the three o'clock at Aintree then I might not be quite so magnetic. But Gran says if Mum wasn't so busy answering phones for Dr. Cement, who is her boss and who has bulgy eyes like hard-boiled eggs (which is why everyone calls him Dr. Bugeye), and Dad wasn't so busy solving crises at the council, then they would be able to solve some crises at 73 Rollins Road, i.e. our house. So you see it is completely not my fault.

For instance, the **DISASTER** with Rooney, who is our class rat, might not have even been such a **DISASTER** if it wasn't for several many **OTHER** people, i.e.:

1. Georgia May Morton-Jones,

who is my cousin, and who should NOT have brought round her real leather briefcase with two compartments and a secret slot.

b. Lilya Bobylev, who is Georgia May Morton-Jones's au pair, and who should have taken an aspirin after all.

3. Cosmo Moon Webster, who is my best friend (even though he is a boy and exactly a week older than me), and who should not have made the **AMAZING MAZE**.

iv) Dad, who is my dad, who should not have claimed he was a **RESPONSIBLE ADULT**, because as Mum says, he is **CLEARLY NOT**.

e. Miss Patterson, who is our class teacher and very tall and thin like a beanpole, and who should have got a guinea pig after all.

But it was a **DISASTER**, and this is why…

What happens is that Mr. Schumann, who is
our headmaster, and who is mostly saying
things like **"Penelope Jones, for the
umpteenth time will you please sit with
your bottom on the chair and your feet on
the floor and NOT the other way round"**,
says something different, i.e. that our class is
allowed a pet, and we will
all take turns to look after it at
weekends, and it will teach us
about **RESPONSIBILITY**,
and a guinea
pig would be
a good idea.

Only then Miss Patterson decides that the pet should teach us about **TOLERANCE** as well, i.e. we should get an animal that is **UNPOPULAR FOR NO GOOD REASON**. So then everyone starts to have **BRILLIANT IDEAS™** about what pet to get, e.g. Luke Bruce thinks we should get a shark and Cosmo thinks we

should get a Tyrannosaurus rex. Only Miss Patterson says **a)** we cannot fit a shark into the classroom,

and **b)** Tyrannosauruses
are **EXTINCT** and **DEAD**.

So Bridget Grimes,
who is top of the
class and Mr.
Schumann's favourite,
says we should get a rat,

because they are actually **CLEAN** and **CLEVER**
(i.e. like her) and Miss Patterson agrees and the
next day there is a rat in a glass tank where the
locusts used to be (which is another story
entirely). And then Miss Patterson says we can
each put a name in a hat (only it is not a hat,
it is an old paint pot), and she will pull one out
and that is what we will call him, and it has to
be a boy's name because it is a boy rat, so no
*Princess*es please. So I put in *Ichabod* (which is

what my dad wanted to call
me only Mum said no
because it is too weird
and also I am not a
boy), and Cosmo
puts in *Flame.*

Only Miss Patterson does not pull those names out she pulls out

which was Henry Potts's idea. So Cosmo gets cross because Henry Potts is his mortal enemy and he throws a rubber at him, and Henry throws a pencil tin back and it hits Rooney's glass tank and Rooney squeaks, and they both get sent to Mr. Schumann.

Mr. Schumann says their punishment is that they are **DISQUALIFIED** from looking after Rooney until they can learn some **RESPONSIBILITY**. Only Cosmo says Rooney is supposed to be teaching them **RESPONSIBILITY**, so if they don't look after him how can they learn it? And Henry Potts agrees (even though he is a mortal enemy), and also says Mr. Schumann is being **INTOLERANT**.

Only Mr. Schumann does not agree and says

they will be disqualified for ever if they do not **PIPE DOWN**. Which they do, and they decide that Mr. Schumann is their mortal enemy for the moment and they will not throw rubbers at each other for at least an hour and a bit.

★ ☆ ✦ ✦

So then Miss Patterson makes the rest of us write our own names on pieces of paper and put those into the hat that is not a hat,

and she will pull one name out and that is who will get Rooney for the first weekend, and unbelievably it is **MY NAME**, i.e. Penelope Jones. And I can tell Bridget Grimes is not pleased about this, and nor is Miss Patterson, only she says maybe the **RESPONSIBILITY** will do me good.

And I think maybe **TOLERANCE** will do her good, but I do not say it because I do not want to get sent to Mr. Schumann and be **DISQUALIFIED**.

Only when I get home on Friday with Rooney in the glass tank it is clear that Mum is not pleased either, because she says she is up to **HERE** with Barry (who is Gran's cat, and who has eaten the last of the cheese again, even though Mum has told Gran it is **CAT BISCUITS AND CAT BISCUITS ONLY**), and Daisy (who is my sister, and is very irritating, and who says she will die if she doesn't get a pony like Lucy B. Finnegan), and so the last thing she needs is more animal hoo-ha, especially with a filthy rat. So I tell her he is not filthy, he is in fact **CLEAN** and **CLEVER**,

and amazingly
Dad agrees
and he helps
me set up a
special maze for
Rooney with toilet
rolls and a cat
biscuit in the
middle, and
Rooney solves it
in thirty-three
seconds, which is
faster than Barry
(who just eats a
raisin he finds
on the floor).

And everyone agrees Rooney is a brilliant pet and **COMPLETELY CLEVER**, although Daisy says a pony would be **CLEANER** because ponies do not poo on your hand, which is true. And then I say it is time to put Rooney away because it is not just about **TOLERANCE** it is about **RESPONSIBILITY**.

And I prove I am utterly responsible because I do not let Rooney sleep in my bed that night, or investigate outside the window in the morning, or make friends with Barry, even though I have seen it on *Animal SOS* (which is a TV series where animals are always nearly dying but then they don't and it is **MIRACULOUS**), because Gran says Barry is not tolerant of anyone (e.g. the man who does the news), and so he is not likely to be friends with a rat, plus Barry is a brilliant hunter and will pounce on Rooney and murder him. So I responsibly keep Rooney in his glass tank in my bedroom and I feed him my cereal through the wire on the top, which is what we are doing when the doorbell goes.

It is my cousin Georgia May Morton-Jones,
with her au pair, Lilya Bobylev, who asks
Mum if she can look after Georgia May
because she has to see Dr. Cement about her
earache. Aunt Deedee, who is Georgia May's
mum and is usually shouting on the phone

to the **NEW YORK BOYS**, says pain is all in the mind and that when she broke her arm she only took an aspirin and did three conference calls and sacked Miss Fazakerley-Knowles before she went to hospital. Only Lilya says the pain is not all in her mind it is all in her ear. But Mum says she can't look after Georgia May because she has to see Dr. Cement, only not for earache, for filing, and Gran is not allowed to look after Georgia May except in **END OF THE WORLD EMERGENCIES** because of the time Georgia May shaved all her hair off. So Dad says **HE** will look after her, because he is a **RESPONSIBLE ADULT** and anyway, how hard can it be? And I can tell Mum is about to say something about that, and possibly so is Georgia May, but then the phone goes and it is Lucy B. Finnegan asking if Daisy can come horse riding, so then Mum has to find Daisy's jodhpurs and drop her off at the stables on the way to Dr. Cement's so it is agreed that Dad will be in charge.

Normally I am completely **GLOOMY** when Georgia May comes to play because she is only four and a bit, and not at all interested in my

BRILLIANT IDEAS™

in case they ruin her clothes or her fingers
(which are very important because
Mr. Nakamura says she shows potential
on the violin). Only this time I have Rooney,
and Georgia May is quite excited because she
has learned lots of interesting rat facts in
biological science at The Drabble Academy
for Girls,
e.g. that
rats see
with their
whiskers
and keep cool
with their tails.

Home work on RATS

hot

Keeping cool

Seeing with whiskers

We do not have biological science at St Regina's, we have nature walks (only not at the moment because Miss Patterson says she is not taking anyone into Hooton Copse again until I can be trusted not to fall out of a tree). Anyway, we are about to test if Rooney can see with his whiskers, when it turns out that Mum was wrong because Dad is suddenly **VERY RESPONSIBLE** and says we are not allowed to let Rooney wander around the floor, in case of **UNFORESEEN CIRCUMSTANCES**, e.g. Barry. Only Georgia May says they are not **UNFORESEEN** because he has just **FORESEEN** them, but Dad says he is not getting into an argument about words, because in fact he could have been a professor if he hadn't married Mum. But Georgia May says no he could not, because he does not have a real leather briefcase, he has a pink rucksack with a picture of a princess on it (which in fact he borrowed from Daisy because Barry chewed his black one). And Dad says it is not essential to have a real leather briefcase to be a professor and Georgia May says yes it is, which is why Aunt Deedee bought her one yesterday, and she shows it to him, and it is very definitely real leather, plus it has two compartments and a secret slot. Which is when I have my

which is to turn her briefcase into a portable rat carrier, and we can put Rooney in the secret slot and his food in one of the compartments and his bed in the other.

Only Georgia May Morton-Jones does not think this is so **BRILLIANT** because Rooney will poo on the leather, and Dad looks like he possibly agrees, only the doorbell goes again so he has to answer it. And this time it is Cosmo Moon Webster, who has come to be **RESPONSIBLE** and **TOLERANT** with Rooney too.

Then Dad has one of his

(which are like **BRILLIANT** ones, only Mum almost never thinks they are **BRIGHT** or **BRILLIANT**), which is to make pizza for everyone for lunch. Only we don't have any cheese, because Barry has eaten it, so Dad says he will go to the shop and Gran can be in charge and it will only be for an hour and Aunt Deedee will never know.

So for a while we are totally responsible, i.e. we watch *Animal SOS* with Gran (only Georgia May keeps her eyes shut because there is a monkey who miraculously **DOES NOT DIE** even though another monkey has bitten his arm and it is hanging off, and also because she is only allowed to watch the Maths Channel). But then Cosmo notices that Gran is fast asleep and says maybe it would be **RESPONSIBLE** to go upstairs and do something quiet, e.g. make Rooney a new and **IMPROVED** maze.

And we do, and it is an **AMAZING** maze,

because you start on the Pirate's Ship (which is

actually a shoebox with some sails),

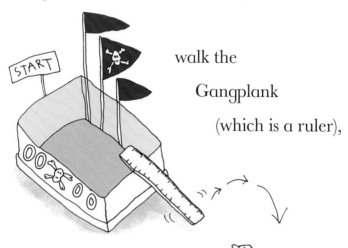

walk the

Gangplank

(which is a ruler),

dive into the

Shark-Infested Waters

(which is actually an old

biscuit tin with some plastic animals in),

then go through the Catacombs of Death

(which is fourteen toilet rolls joined up in a tube),

and into the Haunted House (which is Daisy's doll's house), up the mini stairs, out the mini bathroom window

and into the Prize Arena (which is the glass tank), where there is a chocolate digestive for a prize (because for once Barry has eaten all the cat biscuits).

And Rooney is obviously as clever as a professor even without a real leather briefcase, because he goes along the Gangplank, into the

Shark-Infested Waters – where he actually attacks a hammerhead (i.e. a plastic sheep) – then goes into the Catacombs of Death. Only the catacombs fall apart because Cosmo has trodden on them accidentally, and so I help Rooney a bit by putting him through the front door of the Haunted House.

And **THAT** is where the **DISASTER** begins, i.e. Rooney does not come out of the bathroom

window. In fact he does not come out **AT ALL**.
So Cosmo says he has probably just decided to
have a sleep in the genuine oak miniature
four-poster bed with lace canopy. Only then
ten minutes have gone and he is still not awake,
and when we open up the front of the house the
genuine oak miniature four-poster bed only has
three posters left, and there is a big hole in the
wall, and Rooney is nowhere to be seen,

i.e. he is not in the

Catacombs

of Death, or

in the Pirate

Ship, or

even in my

bedroom.

So then Cosmo says maybe we should use Barry to sniff Rooney out, only we will capture Rooney with an ice-cream tub before Barry pounces and murders him. Only Barry is not too keen on getting up from the sofa because he is watching a programme about bees, so Cosmo gives him the chocolate digestive prize and he is keener all of a sudden.

And he does some sniffing
in my room and he finds
a lot of things, e.g.:

a) An old sock

2. A piece of liquorice

c. A dead fly

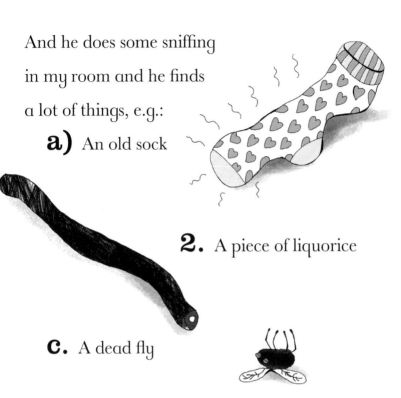

But **NO ROONEY**. Cosmo says he has probably
fled to his freedom, which is a **GOOD THING**,
because Cosmo's mum (who is called Sunflower,
even though her real name is Barbara) does not
believe in keeping animals locked in cages

because it is **AGAINST THEIR RIGHTS**. But I
do not think this is a **GOOD THING** and nor
will Miss Patterson and so I am suddenly very
gloomy, which is when Dad gets back with the
cheese and says, **"Why the long face, Jones?"**

And so I tell him, and amazingly instead
of telling me I am **IRRESPONSIBLE**, he says,

"He'll be in the plumbing. Rats always are."

And he gets a wrench and a pair of pliers,
and says,

Did I ever tell you I could have
been a plumber if I hadn't
met your mother?

Only I do not think this is true because he unscrews a bit of pipe and water bursts all over everyone, which is when Mum and Daisy and Lilya Bobylev all walk in.

And then it is **MAYHEM** because Georgia May Morton-Jones is crying like **MAD** because she says she will catch a cold and will miss her violin exam and Mr. Nakamura will be disappointed in her,

and Lilya Bobylev is crying like **MAD** because Aunt Deedee will sack her for making Mr. Nakamura disappointed in Georgia May, and Daisy is crying like **MAD** because the wet has flooded her chewed-up doll's house. And she says,

It is ALL YOUR FAULT, Penelope Jones.

Only Mum (who has gone a bit palish and her lips are very thin), says it is not my fault, it is **DAD'S**, and he has proved that he is **NOT** a **RESPONSIBLE ADULT** and that it is the last time she is **EVER** leaving him in charge.

But even though she says it is not my fault I am still completely gloomy because I do not think Bridget Grimes or Miss Patterson or Mr. Schumann will agree when I go to school on Monday with no Rooney.

But then Dad has another of his

which is to go to Paradise Pets and buy a new rat that looks just like Rooney and **NO ONE WILL BE ANY THE WISER**. And Mum says this is really **NOT BRIGHT** because we are bound to get found out, only Dad does not agree and Mum says **"Fine"** because she has to sort out the pipes and Daisy's doll's house and some dry clothes for Georgia May Morton-Jones.

And so that is what we do. We buy a new rat called Rooney 2 and he looks just the same and so Dad is right – **NO ONE WILL BE ANY THE WISER**.

Especially not Miss Patterson, who is completely pleased when I come in on Monday with the glass tank and Rooney 2 inside it, and she says I have **"proved my critics wrong"**, i.e. Bridget Grimes.

Only Bridget Grimes does not like being proved wrong, and in history, when we are supposed to be learning about King Alfred who burned some cakes, she is staring very hard at Rooney and says,

Miss Patterson, Miss, why is Rooney so fat? I think Penelope Jones has been feeding him irresponsible things and he is obese and will die.

Only for once Miss Patterson does not agree and reminds her about **INTOLERANCE** and makes her go and sit in the corner with Alexander Pringle, who is in trouble for eating peanut butter sandwiches in class again.

And so I am just thinking that **DISASTER** has been **AVERTED** when it gets **VERTED** again, i.e. on Wednesday morning we go into class and Rooney has had eight rat babies. And I say it is a **MIRACLE** because Rooney is a boy.

Only Miss Patterson does not agree that it is **MIRACULOUS** and she sends me to Mr. Schumann, where I have to explain about the maze, and the pipes, and Rooney 2. But, like I tell him, it is not my fault, it is just that I am a **MAGNET FOR DISASTER**. Only Mr. Schumann does not agree and I am banned from learning about **RESPONSIBILITY** for the rest of the year, and so is anyone else until he can work out what to do with all the rat babies. So everyone else starts being very **INTOLERANT** because they do not get to look after Rooney 2 at all and Henry Potts says I have **IRRESPONSIBLY** lost Rooney 1 who has probably been eaten by **INTOLERANT** wolves or jaguars. And Cosmo says jaguars do not eat rats they eat boys called

Potts, and then Henry Potts says he is being **INTOLERANT**, and Cosmo says Henry is being **INTOLERANT** and then Miss Patterson tells everyone to stop the **INTOLERANCE NONSENSE** and open up their art books.

Only when I get home, I find out that I have not lost Rooney 1 and he has not been eaten by jaguars or wolves, he is back at Paradise Pets. What happened was he had been **ASLEEP** in the secret slot in Georgia May Morton-Jones's real leather briefcase. Only he woke up in her violin exam and bit Mr. Nakamura who was very **INTOLERANT** and failed Georgia May. And I know this because Aunt Deedee rings Mum to shout about the filthy rat.

But Mum tells Aunt Deedee that in fact rats are not filthy, they are **CLEAN** and **CLEVER**, and she should be more **TOLERANT**.

But Aunt Deedee says there is such a thing as **TOO MUCH TOLERANCE**, which is why Georgia May is on Grade 4 violin and I can't even play "Twinkle Twinkle Little Star" on the

recorder without getting several notes wrong.
So then Mum says something **INTOLERANT**
and **IRRESPONSIBLE** and Aunt Deedee puts
the phone down.

And I say in fact it is good that Mum
thinks rats are **CLEAN** and **CLEVER**,
because Mr. Schumann has actually had a
BRILLIANT IDEA™, which is that we can
take a rat baby to look after at home, but
only if we get **PERMISSION IN WRITING**. Only
Mum says she is up to here with rat nonsense,
and even if they could use the toilet and wash
their hands she is not giving
me **PERMISSION**

IN WRITING to

have a rat baby.

Daisy says, **"It is all your fault,**
Penelope Jones, you are such a complete
numpty." But it is not my fault. It is just
that I am a

Magnet
for
Disaster.

Only now I think
about it, maybe it is
all Aunt Deedee's fault.
Because she is the one
who bought the real
leather briefcase
in the first place.

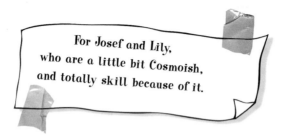

For Josef and Lily,
who are a little bit Cosmoish,
and totally skill because of it.

Published by Pearson Education Limited, Edinburgh Gate, Harlow, Essex, CM20 2JE.
www.pearsonschools.co.uk

Text © Joanna Nadin, 2011
Cover artwork and inside illustrations used by permission of Usborne Publishing Limited.
Copyright © 2011 Usborne Publishing Limited
Illustrated by Jess Mikhail

The right of Joanna Nadin to be identified as author of this work has been asserted by her in accordance with
the Copyright, Designs and Patents Act 1988.

First published as part of *Penny Dreadful is a Complete CATastrophe* by Usborne Publishing Limited in 2011.
This educational edition first published by Pearson Education Limited in 2014.

17 16 15
10 9 8 7 6 5 4 3

British Library Cataloguing in Publication Data
A catalogue record for this book is available from the British Library

ISBN 978 0 435 16049 4

Printed in Slovakia by Neografia

Acknowledgements
Every effort has been made to contact copyright holders of material reproduced in this book. Any omissions
will be rectified in subsequent printings if notice is given to the publishers.

This is a special edition of this book for Wordsmith.
To order further copies please contact:
Telephone: 0845 630 22 22
Fax: 0845 313 77 77
Email: customer.orders@pearson.com
Web: www.pearsonprimary.co.uk/wordsmith